D1243757

The Two O'Clock Secret

The Two O'Clock Secret

BETHANY ROBERTS   illustrated by ROBIN KRAMER

ALBERT WHITMAN & COMPANY • Morton Grove, Illinois

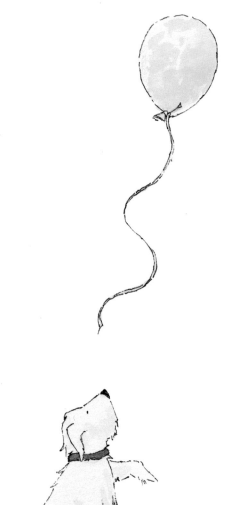

The text is typeset in Palatino.
The illustrations are watercolor and ink.

Library of Congress Cataloging-in-Publication Data
Roberts, Bethany
The two o'clock secret/Bethany Roberts;
illustrated by Robin Kramer.
p. cm.
Summary: Little Michael has a hard time keeping
his father's wonderful birthday secret.
ISBN 0-8075-8159-3
[1. Birthdays—Fiction. 2. Fathers—Fiction.
3. Secrets—Fiction.] I. Kramer, Robin, ill.
II. Title.
PZ7.R5396Tw 1993   92-6405
[E]—dc20   CIP
                                          AC

Text © 1993 by Barbara Beverage.
Illustrations © 1993 by Robin Kramer.
Published in 1993 by Albert Whitman & Company,
6340 Oakton, Morton Grove, Illinois 60053-2723.
Published simultaneously in Canada by
General Publishing, Limited, Toronto.
10 9 8 7 6 5 4 3 2 1

There's a birthday surprise,
and I can't tell,
but it's hard,
it's hard
to keep a secret.

"Now, Michael, *don't tell.*
Don't tell your father
like you did last year."
(All that I'd said was,
"We got you a shirt,
but you don't know what color!")

"And remember the time
he told about Jasper?
He blew *that* one, too,"
says my sister, Kate.
(All that I'd done was
point to a dog and say,
"I know a surprise
who looks like that!")

Dad only laughs.
"You're just like my brother—
he always tells secrets."
Then Dad looks sad.
(Uncle Jim's in the Navy,
and we haven't seen him
for over two years.)
Mom gives me a wink
because Dad doesn't know
the surprise we have,
and I can't tell,
but it's hard,
it's hard
to keep a secret!

Mom called the airlines.
Kate wrote some letters.
I put the stamps on

and biked to the mailbox.
One letter was special.
(Won't Dad be surprised!)

We went to the store
and bought lots of presents,

then wrapped them up
in bright, happy paper.

Now they're hidden from sight
in the dark hall closet.
But the best one of all—
the two o'clock secret—
just can't be wrapped!

Kate made a sign
that says HAPPY BIRTHDAY!
Mom did some baking,
and I licked the beaters.

We made newspaper hats
and newspaper airplanes,
and blew up big balloons.
(They're all in my room
where Dad won't look.)
And I can't tell,
and I can't *wait*
till it's time for the secret!

Now the clock chimes two.
Jasper barks, "WOOF!"
and looks out the window.
"What's wrong with you, fella?"
calls Dad from his chair.
"Oh, it's nothing!" I say.
"Just a cat,
or some traffic."

But Dad opens the door.
There are Gram and Aunt Alice
and Great-Uncle Fred.
"SURPRISE!" we all shout.
And standing right behind,
with carrot-red hair
and a smile just like Dad's,
is my tall Uncle Jim!

First Dad just stares.
Then he cries, "Ohmigosh!"
"Hey, Brother," he yells.
"Hey, Twin!" yells my uncle,
and they look like two mirrors!

There are hugs all around,
and we sing "Happy Birthday"
while Gram plays the piano.
Then Mom lights the candles
of *two* chocolate cakes!
"A *two-birthday* secret,"
my dad says to me.
"And you didn't tell,
not even a hint!"

Then my tall Uncle Jim
lifts me high in the air.
It was hard not to tell,
it was hard,
it was hard,
but...*I kept the secret!*